CHRISTIANE DUCHESNE

DORIS BARRETTE

Who's Afraid of The Dark?

Scholastic Canada Ltd.

Scholastic Canada Ltd.
175 Hillmount Road, Markham, Ontario L6C 1Z7
Scholastic Inc.
555 Broadway, New York, NY 10012, USA
Scholastic Australia Pty Limited
PO Box 579, Gosford, NSW 2250, Australia
Scholastic New Zealand Limited
Private Bag 94407, Greenmount, Auckland, New Zealand
Scholastic Ltd.
Villiers House, Clarendon Avenue, Leamington Spa,
Warwickshire CV32 5PR, UK

English text by
David Homel

The illustrations in this book were painted in watercolour on
illustration board. The artist develops her dynamic range of colours
by building thin layers of paint on a wet or dry surface.

Canadian Cataloguing in Publication Data
Duchesne, Christiane, 1949-
[Qui a peur, la nuit? English]
Who's afraid of the dark?

Translation of: Qui a peur, la nuit?
ISBN 0-590-03841-9

I. Barrette, Doris. II. Title. III. Title: Qui a peur, la nuit? English

PS8557.U265Q513 1998   jC843'.54   C98-931142-2
PZ7.D83Wh 1998

5 4 3 2 1   Printed and bound in Canada   8 9/9 0 1 2 3 4 /0

For Julia and Alexis.
C.D.

To Benjamin.
D.B.

●

At sunrise, Maurice the cat stepped outside to stretch and to check the weather. Before long, the mystery cats appeared through the mist.

These cats had no homes, and they belonged to no-one. They lived in the field behind the house. They had no names of their own, so Maurice called them Bruiser, Stripes, Skinny and Little Tail.

Maurice said to his friends, "In the darkness, there are shades and shadows. Last night, I saw the shadow of a gigantic cat on the kitchen wall — an enormous, growling monster that eats cats like us for breakfast!"

"Weren't you afraid?" Skinny asked.

"I'm never afraid," declared Maurice.

"Really?" said Little Tail. "Say, Maurice, would you happen to have something to eat?"

Maurice went inside and came back with five cookies for breakfast. Then the cats wrestled and dozed and climbed trees until nightfall.

The next day the
mystery cats appeared
again. They warmed
themselves in the sun
for a few moments.
Then Maurice spoke.

"In the darkness," he
began, "There are ghosts.
Last night, I saw three ghosts playing violins. And
you know what? They didn't make a sound!"

"Weren't you afraid?" asked Bruiser.

"I'm never afraid," declared Maurice.

"Is that so?" said Stripes. "Say, Maurice,
would you happen to have a little something
to snack on?"

Maurice went inside and returned with five
pieces of French bread. Then they chased
each other down to the riverbank and
explored among the rocks until nightfall.

The next morning, as the wind blew around them, Maurice said, "In the dark, I can hear the house moaning and groaning. Last night, the staircase creaked all by itself. Everyone was asleep, but I heard the steps making horrible noises!"

8

"Weren't you afraid?" the others cried.

"I'm never afraid!" insisted Maurice.

"Say, Maurice . . ."

"Yes, I'll go find us something to eat," said Maurice.

"No, that's not it," said Little Tail.

"There's something we need to talk to you about," added Bruiser.

"Maurice," Little Tail began in a small voice, "in the dark, we get really scared."

"Brave cats like you? You're afraid of the dark?"

"We are!" said the four cats, with one voice.

Maurice burst out laughing. "But why?" he asked.

They glanced at each other.

"Sometimes storms crash over our heads!" said Stripes.

"Sometimes the trees move around us!" said Bruiser.

"Sometimes there are strange noises, growling in the dark!" said Skinny.

"And you're really afraid of all that?" wondered Maurice.

"We are!" they cried.

Maurice opened his eyes wide and stared at them. "But what could happen to you?"

"Rivers of water might fall from the sky to drown us," said Skinny.

12

"The trees might begin to walk and crush us,"
said Stripes.

"Catnappers could be hiding in the dark to steal
us," said Little Tail.

"And we're afraid of being afraid!" Bruiser finished.

That night, Maurice couldn't sleep. He pictured his friends lying under a tree out in the field. He pictured them trembling with fear and keeping a wary watch for monsters and catnappers.

"Maybe I should go look for them," he said to himself. "I could sing them a lullaby. I could lick them behind the ears . . . Maybe they'd feel better."

Outside in the darkness, all was quiet and mysterious. Maurice tiptoed across the field. Where did they sleep? Where could they be hiding? To keep from scaring them, he called out very softly, "Stripes? Little Tail? Where are you?

16

Bruiser, say something! Oh, Skinny, are you out there?"

Suddenly a flash of lightning split the sky and a crash of thunder sent Maurice dashing across the field.

17

"The sky is opening! The clouds are exploding!
The trees are walking!" screamed Maurice. "I hear
the monsters and the catnappers! Help me!

"My house has disappeared, I'm lost!" he
wailed as the rain pelted down harder
and harder.

Maurice ran blindly, but his paws seemed to know the way. Before he knew it, he was back on the big wooden porch, soaked to the skin and trembling with fear.

"Maurice!"

He opened his eyes.

"It's you!" Maurice cried. His friends sat on the porch before him.

"We were so scared tonight," Skinny whispered. "It was awful out there!"

"We saw the trees racing through the fields!" said Bruiser.

"We saw your house disappear in the storm!" said Stripes.

"We saw your monster, your ghosts and the catnapper!" added Little Tail.

"We were so frightened that we came to find you!" said Little Tail.

"We saw you running across the fields," said Stripes.

"Weren't you afraid?" Bruiser asked.

"You're trembling!" Skinny exclaimed.

"Oh, yes, I was afraid," said Maurice. He stopped for a moment to lick his paw. "I was very afraid . . . for you."

24

Lightning was still cutting blue slashes through the sky as Maurice let them all into the house.

"Don't make any noise," he said to his friends. "Come along, my blanket is big enough for everyone."

They fell asleep together, exhausted by the storm, snuggling up for warmth.

The next morning, while the other cats were still fast asleep, Maurice stepped outside just before dawn to see what sort of day it would be.

Gazing out across the fields, he thought about the night before. "In the darkness," he murmured, "I saw . . ."

But then he stopped.
He didn't want to miss the sunrise.

The End